YOU ARE NOT NECESSARILY A FOOL BECAUSE YOU DIDN'T GO TO SCHOOL.

KNOWLEDGE IS POWER.

YOU NEED IT EVERY HOUR.

READ A BOOK!

DISCARD

You go on to school. There are things you can learn from your teachers, but don't you stop thinking for yourself. AND DON'T YOU STOP ASKING QUESTIONS.

WORDS. THAT'S WHY PEOPLE NEED OUR BOOKSTORE.

Carolrhoda Books
A division of Lerner Publishing Group, Inc.
241 First Avenue North
Minneapolis, MN 55401 USA

For reading levels and more information, look up this title at www.lernerbooks.com.

Main body text Bailey Sans ITC Std. Typeface provided by International Typeface Corp.

Library of Congress Cataloging-in-Publication Data

The Cataloging-in-Publication Data for *The Book Itch: Freedom, Truth & Harlem's Greatest Bookstore* is on file at the Library of Congress.
ISBN 978-0-7613-3943-4 (lib. bdg. : alk. paper)
ISBN 978-1-4677-4618-2 (eBook)

Manufactured in the United States of America
1 – DP – 7/15/15

For Lewis H. Michaux Jr.
and his remarkable father
—v.m.n.

For "Brotherman" Samatar Egag
—r.g.c.

The BOOK ITCH

FREEDOM, TRUTH & HARLEM'S GREATEST BOOKSTORE

Vaunda Micheaux NELSON

ILLUSTRATED BY R. Gregory CHRISTIE

CAROLRHODA BOOKS • MINNEAPOLIS

"THIS HOUSE IS PACKED WITH ALL THE FACTS ABOUT ALL THE BLACKS ALL OVER THE WORLD."

That's what it says above our door. We own this place, this house—the National Memorial African Bookstore. It's our home, just about, because we spend so much time here.

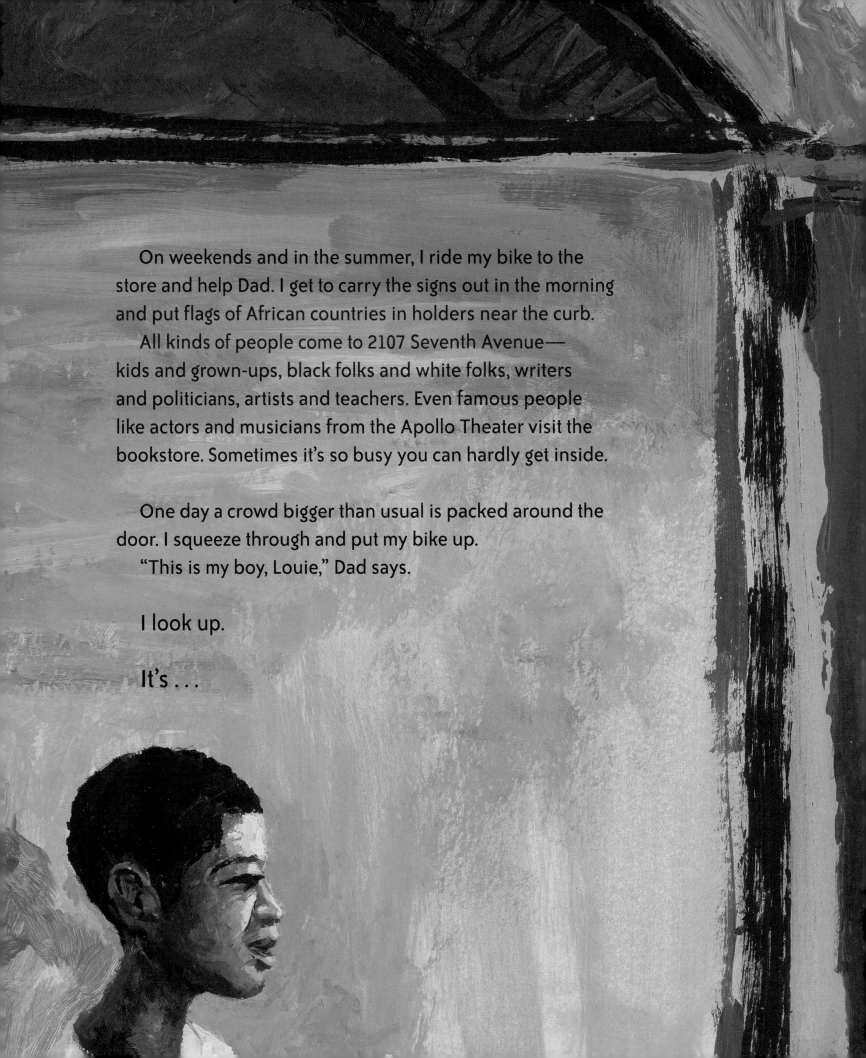

On weekends and in the summer, I ride my bike to the store and help Dad. I get to carry the signs out in the morning and put flags of African countries in holders near the curb.

All kinds of people come to 2107 Seventh Avenue— kids and grown-ups, black folks and white folks, writers and politicians, artists and teachers. Even famous people like actors and musicians from the Apollo Theater visit the bookstore. Sometimes it's so busy you can hardly get inside.

One day a crowd bigger than usual is packed around the door. I squeeze through and put my bike up.

"This is my boy, Louie," Dad says.

I look up.

It's . . .

It's MUHAMMAD ALI!

He's so tall, I have to lean my head way back to see his face. I feel his big boxer's fingers close over mine. It's like shaking hands with a giant. I can't think of anything to say.

Mr. Ali pushes my chin up. I guess my mouth was hanging wide open. He and Dad are laughing at me, but I don't care. I just met the heavyweight champion of the world!

Dad opened his store in Harlem Square way before I was born. Mom says he started out with five books. Five books and a mission. She says he had something in his heart he believed in so much that he'd do just about anything to make it happen.

Dad says he got the book itch and needed to scratch it.

Back then, he'd walk up Seventh Avenue and on to 125th Street selling books out of a pushcart.

"DON'T GET TOOK! READ A BOOK!" he'd call.

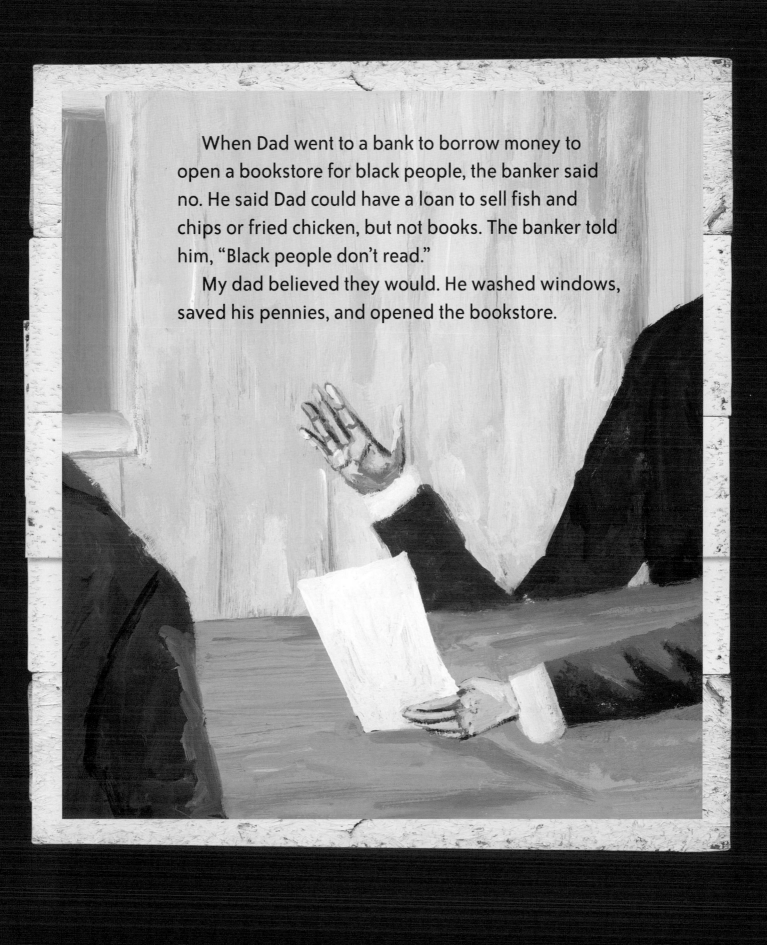

When Dad went to a bank to borrow money to open a bookstore for black people, the banker said no. He said Dad could have a loan to sell fish and chips or fried chicken, but not books. The banker told him, "Black people don't read."

My dad believed they would. He washed windows, saved his pennies, and opened the bookstore.

He was right. People came
AND THEY READ.

Now we have about a zillion books
in the store and more people come
every day. They come and they talk.
They read and they buy.

Dad doesn't have to sell on the street now, but sometimes we do anyway. Dad says he wants to reach people who might not know about the store, people who don't know how important books are.

We push the cart calling,

"KNOWLEDGE IS POWER. YOU NEED IT EVERY HOUR.
READ A BOOK!"

Dad made that up just like he made up the sign over the store. He plays with words until they say what he feels. I guess that makes him a poet.

Dad's name is the same as mine, Lewis Michaux. But people call him the Professor, even though he didn't go to school much. Dad says he doesn't have "college knowledge." He educated himself by reading books and by living.

He says, **"YOU ARE NOT NECESSARILY A FOOL BECAUSE YOU DIDN'T GO TO SCHOOL."**

"Can I stay home and read books and learn by living?" I ask.

"You go on to school," Dad says. "There are things you can learn from your teachers, but don't you stop thinking for yourself.

"AND DON'T YOU STOP ASKING QUESTIONS."

Me and my dad talk about important things. Things like truth and what it means to be free. Dad says books can help you. Not every book is true, he says, but the more you read, the easier it is to figure out for yourself what is true.

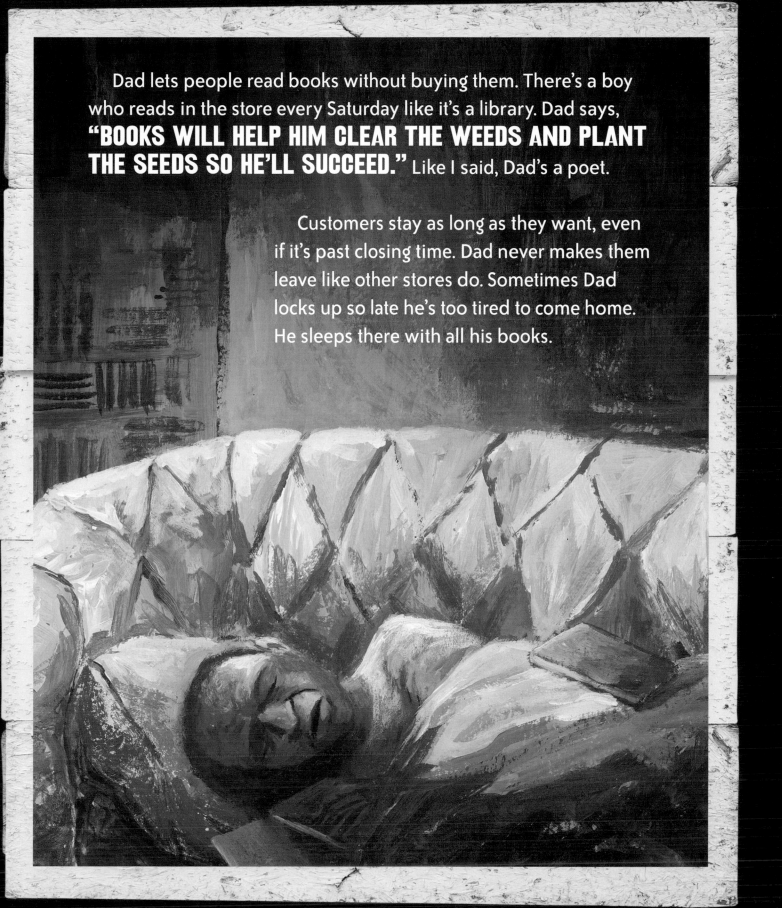

Dad lets people read books without buying them. There's a boy who reads in the store every Saturday like it's a library. Dad says, **"BOOKS WILL HELP HIM CLEAR THE WEEDS AND PLANT THE SEEDS SO HE'LL SUCCEED."** Like I said, Dad's a poet.

Customers stay as long as they want, even if it's past closing time. Dad never makes them leave like other stores do. Sometimes Dad locks up so late he's too tired to come home. He sleeps there with all his books.

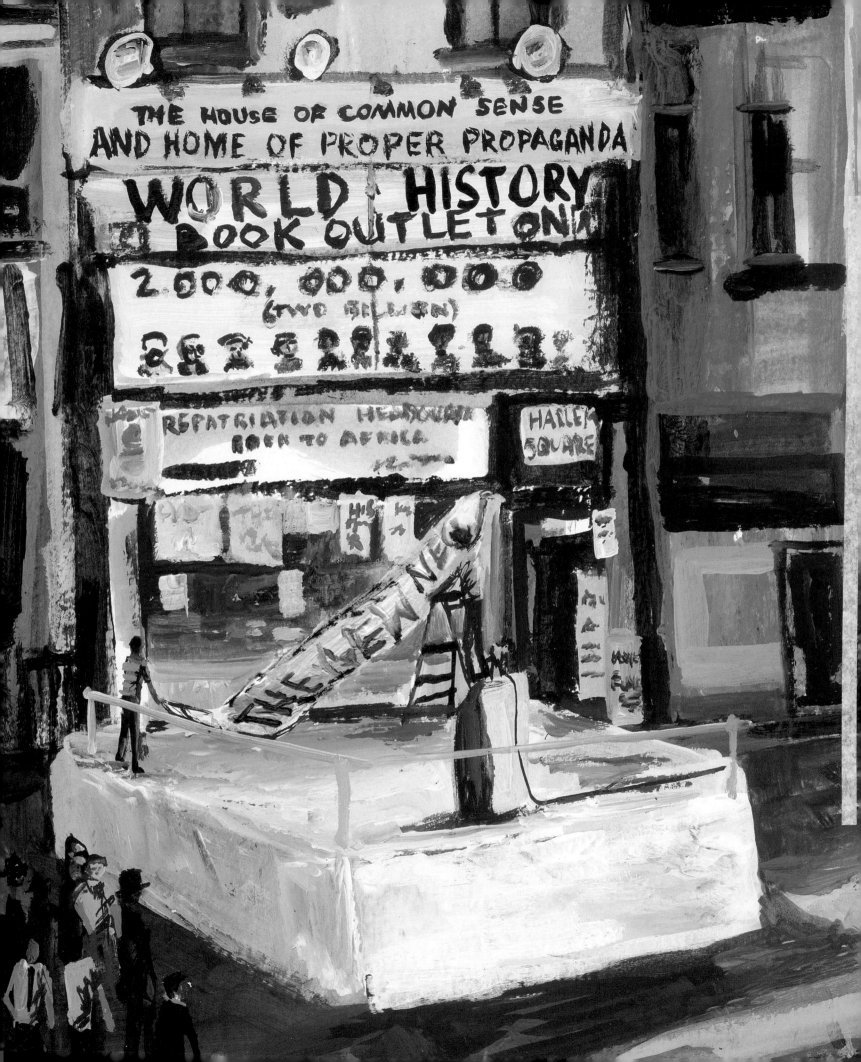

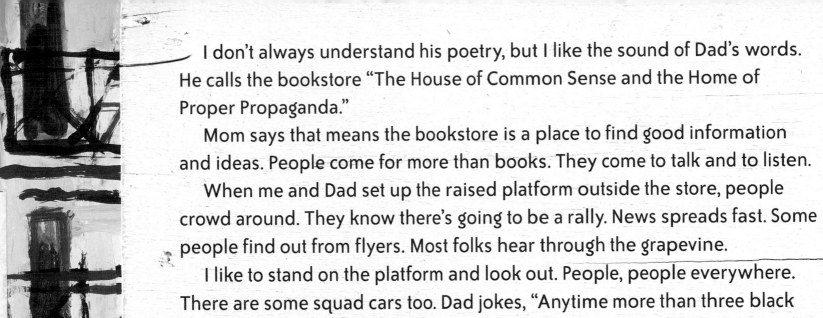

I don't always understand his poetry, but I like the sound of Dad's words. He calls the bookstore "The House of Common Sense and the Home of Proper Propaganda."

Mom says that means the bookstore is a place to find good information and ideas. People come for more than books. They come to talk and to listen.

When me and Dad set up the raised platform outside the store, people crowd around. They know there's going to be a rally. News spreads fast. Some people find out from flyers. Most folks hear through the grapevine.

I like to stand on the platform and look out. People, people everywhere. There are some squad cars too. Dad jokes, "Anytime more than three black people congregate, the police get nervous."

People come to hear talk about fighting for the same rights white people have. Talk about jobs and voting. About how black folks should respect and support each other. People shout angry words. They kid around and laugh. Sometimes I don't get why they're mad or what's so funny.

Dad talks to the crowd from the platform too. He says black people need to learn their history by reading books.

"IF YOU DON'T KNOW AND YOU AIN'T GOT NO DOUGH, THEN YOU CAN'T GO, AND THAT'S FOR SHO."

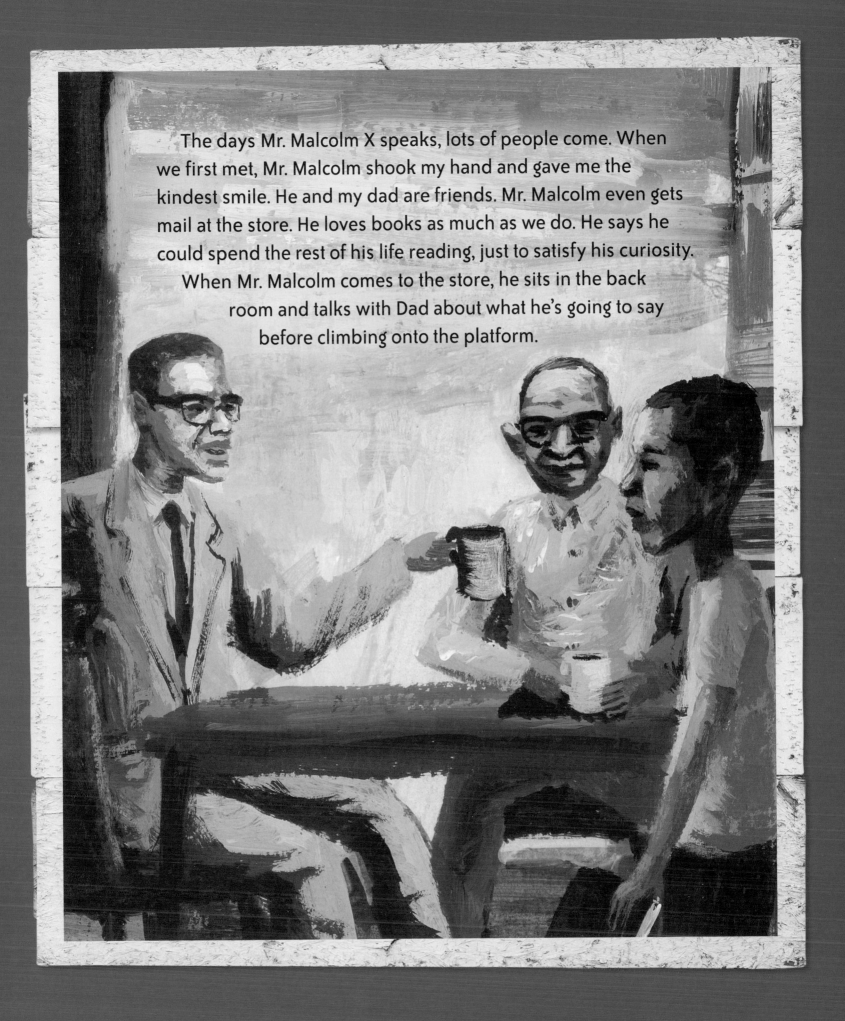

The days Mr. Malcolm X speaks, lots of people come. When we first met, Mr. Malcolm shook my hand and gave me the kindest smile. He and my dad are friends. Mr. Malcolm even gets mail at the store. He loves books as much as we do. He says he could spend the rest of his life reading, just to satisfy his curiosity. When Mr. Malcolm comes to the store, he sits in the back room and talks with Dad about what he's going to say before climbing onto the platform.

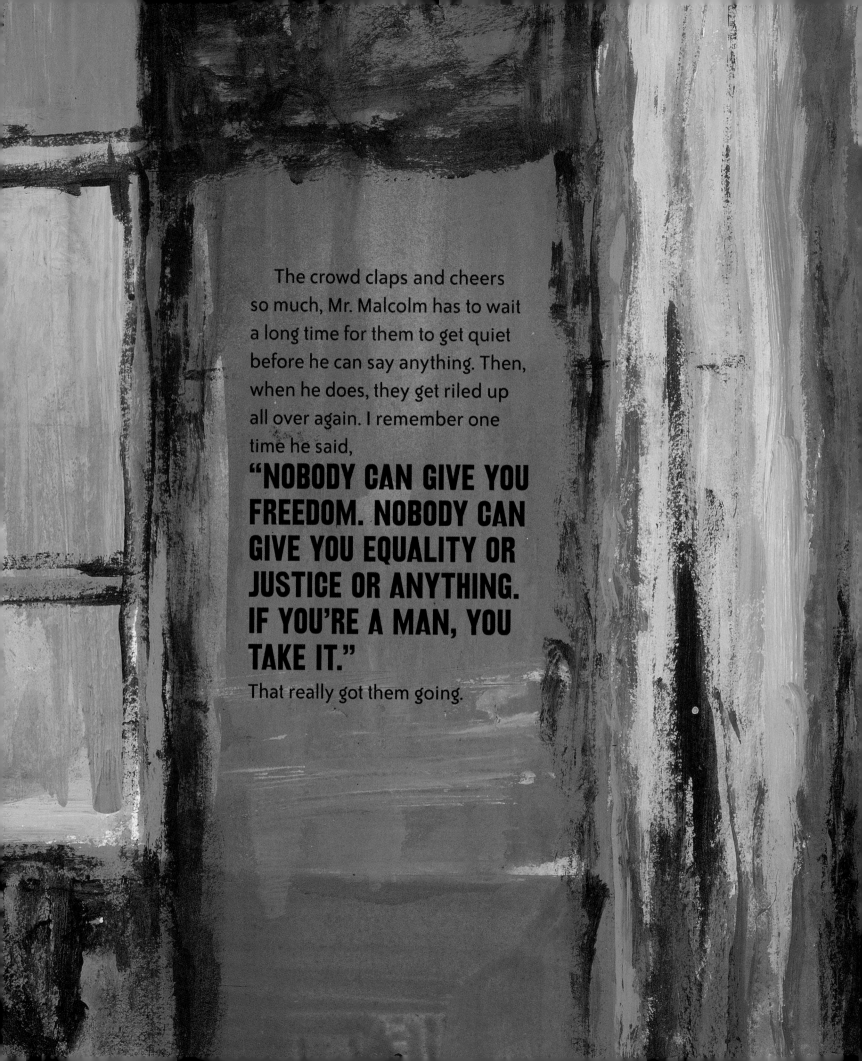

The crowd claps and cheers so much, Mr. Malcolm has to wait a long time for them to get quiet before he can say anything. Then, when he does, they get riled up all over again. I remember one time he said,

"NOBODY CAN GIVE YOU FREEDOM. NOBODY CAN GIVE YOU EQUALITY OR JUSTICE OR ANYTHING. IF YOU'RE A MAN, YOU TAKE IT."

That really got them going.

There are bodyguards watching out for Mr. Malcolm. When I ask Dad why, he says, "Malcolm speaks the truth, and there are people who don't want us to hear it."

One cold day I'm down at Rockefeller Center ice-skating with my friends. When Dad comes for me, he says, "Hurry, now. I have to get up to the Audubon Ballroom. Malcolm's expecting me." I jump in the car, and Dad takes me home. Then he speeds off toward the ballroom.

While I'm doing my homework, Mom gets a phone call. She covers her face and turns away.

Mom hangs up and looks at me. "Malcolm . . ." Her eyes are wet. She can't talk for a minute. "Someone shot him when he stood up to give his speech."

I can't breathe.

Mom opens her arms. I run to her.

"Don't worry," she says, "Your father is coming home."

In. Out. I am breathing again.

Later I hear Dad's key in the door. He hugs Mom and me and sags into his chair. He takes off his glasses and cleans them.

At last he says, "When I got to the ballroom, everybody was rushing out, screaming and hollering. I went inside and there he was, lying dead."

Dad kind of shivers. "I was supposed to be sitting right beside him."

I'm glad he wasn't.

I'm sad they killed Mr. Malcolm. But I'm glad my dad is all right. I'm glad I went skating and Dad came to get me. I'm glad.

After I go to bed, Dad sits in the living room, crying in the dark. I never heard Dad cry before, and I don't know what to do. I can't keep from crying too.

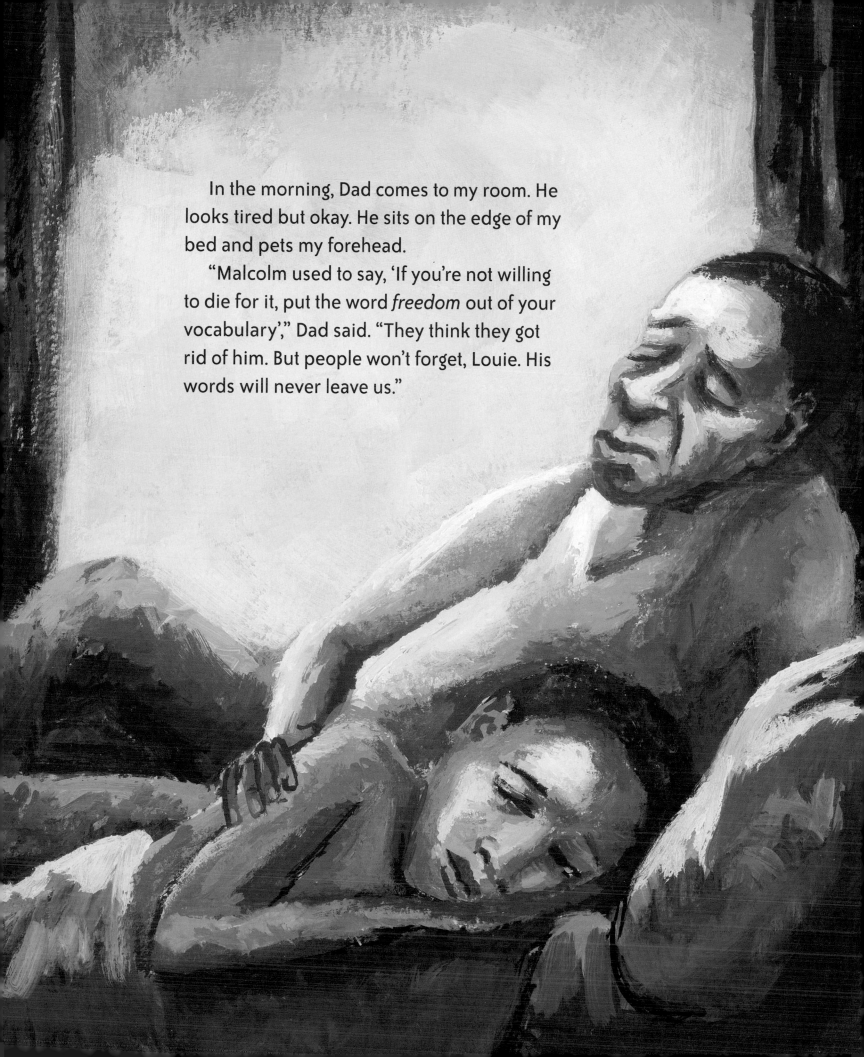

In the morning, Dad comes to my room. He looks tired but okay. He sits on the edge of my bed and pets my forehead.

"Malcolm used to say, 'If you're not willing to die for it, put the word *freedom* out of your vocabulary'," Dad said. "They think they got rid of him. But people won't forget, Louie. His words will never leave us."

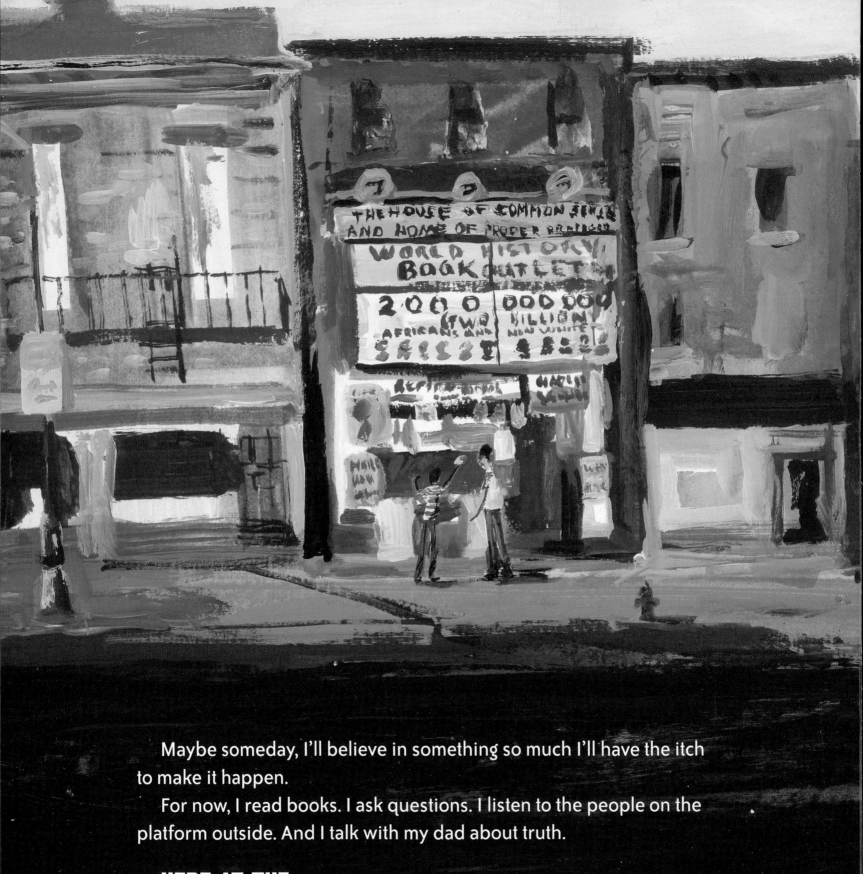

Maybe someday, I'll believe in something so much I'll have the itch to make it happen.

For now, I read books. I ask questions. I listen to the people on the platform outside. And I talk with my dad about truth.

HERE AT THE
NATIONAL MEMORIAL AFRICAN BOOKSTORE.

LEWIS HENRI MICHAUX (1895–1976)

Lewis Michaux was independent-minded from the time he was a child. As a boy, he refused to work in the fields for twenty cents a day. Instead, he found more profitable, sometimes illegal, ways to make money. After some trouble with the law, Lewis became a deacon in his brother's church and ultimately found his calling in books.

Lewis had very little formal education and, at first, knew nothing about the book business, but he was determined to try. He had grown to believe that books could change the lives of black people.

In the early years* of the store, Lewis slept in a back room. He washed windows to make ends meet and walked the streets selling books. Sometimes he was lucky to earn a dollar a day. His dedication paid off. The National Memorial African Bookstore became a Harlem landmark—a gathering place for scholars, politicians, activists, writers, and artists. It would grow to become the nation's largest, most complete center for books by and about black people.

Located near the bustling corner of 125th Street and Seventh Avenue, just around the corner from the Apollo Theater, the store drew such notables as Muhammed Ali, Kwame Nkrumah, W.E.B. DuBois, Louis Armstrong, Nikki Giovanni, Claude McKay, Joe Louis, James Baldwin, Eartha Kitt, and Langston Hughes. Some, like Malcolm X, also spoke at rallies outside the store. Lewis's own strong political and philosophical views were well known, and he gave fiery addresses on black nationalism and the need for blacks to educate themselves about their history. Those who couldn't afford to buy books often were invited into the store to read.

Lewis, known for his wit and candor, referred to his store as "The House of Common Sense and the Home of Proper Propaganda." The community just called it Michaux's. Many visited the store for more than books. They sought stimulating conversation and advice. Over time, Lewis came to be called the Professor.

In 1968, the area of 125th Street and Seventh Avenue was chosen for construction of a new state office building. Some felt that officials had purposely targeted this site to disrupt bookstore activities. Lewis was forced to relocate his store a few blocks down 125th. It remained open for several years until Lewis received notice from the state that he was being evicted. Soon after, he was diagnosed with throat cancer. Lewis closed the doors in 1975 and died August 25, 1976, at the age of eighty-one.**

Lewis Michaux inside his store in the late 1960s

* *The opening date of the bookstore is unclear. Many sources, including Lewis himself, said he sold books for forty-four years, placing the opening about 1931. My research suggests the store began in the late 1930s. However, Lewis may have been selling books prior to opening a storefront.*

** *According to some sources, Lewis was born in 1884 and was in his early nineties when he died, but census records, FBI reports, and a family Bible place his birth year at 1895.*

AUTHOR'S NOTE

I have been researching Lewis Michaux and the National Memorial African Bookstore since the early 1990s. My interest in him and his store is both professional and personal. Lewis Michaux was my great-uncle. I have only one clear memory of visiting the store as a child and, regretfully, didn't realize the store's significance until after it closed and my uncle had passed away.

Transcripts and audio recordings of interviews with Lewis were a strong source in my research, as were articles, books, family archives, and interviews with people who met him, visited the store, or both. A primary source of information and personal experience continues to be Lewis Michaux Jr. He was born late in his father's life and was a young boy during the store's peak years. For this picture book, I chose to imagine his perspective as a way of introducing young readers to the elder Lewis and to the National Memorial African Bookstore.

The bookstore in October 1945

SELECTED BIBLIOGRAPHY

Breitman, George, ed. *Malcolm X Speaks: Selected Speeches and Statements*. New York: Pathfinder, 1989.

Collins, Rodnell P., with A. Peter Bailey. *Seventh Child: A Family Memoir of Malcolm X*. Secaucus, NJ: Carol Pub Group 1998.

"A Conversation with Lewis Michaux, Chester Himes and Nikki Giovanni." *Encore*, September 1972, 46–51.

Davis, Thulani. *Malcolm X: The Great Photograph*s. New York: Stewart, Tabori & Chang, 1993.

Emblidge, David. "Rallying Point: Lewis Michaux's National Memorial African Bookstore." *Publishing Research Quarterly* 24, no. 4 (December 2008),: 267–276.

Goldman, Peter. *The Death and Life of Malcolm X*. 2nd ed. Chicago: University of Illinois Press, 1979.

"Lewis Michaux: The World's Greatest Seller of Black Books." *Third World*. Pts. 1–5. October, 20 1972, 1, 3, 11; November 2, 1972, 3, 13; November 24, 1972, 7, 11–12; December 8, 1972, 3, 13; December 22, 1972, 3, 12.

Michaux, Lewis H. "Dr. Lewis Michaux." Tape-recorded Interview by Michele Wallace, January 18, 1974. Transcript in James V. Hatch, Leo Hamalian, and Judy Blum, eds. *Artist and Influence*. New York: Hatch-Billops Collection, 1997, 120–129.

Michaux, Lewis H. "Louis Michaux, Owner, National Memorial Bookstore." Tape-recorded interview by Robert Wright, July 31, 1970, New York City. The Civil Rights Documentation Project, 1527 New Hampshire Avenue NW, Washington, DC 20036. Transcript: Moorland Spingarn Research Center, Howard University, Washington, DC.

Michaux, Lewis H., Jr. Tape-recorded interview by the author at his home in New York City, August 1999.

X, Malcolm, and Alex Haley. *The Autobiography of Malcolm X*. New York, Ballantine, 1965.

PHOTO ACKNOWLEDGMENTS

Additional images are used with the permission of: courtesy of Vaunda Micheaux Nelson, p. 33; © Ezio Peterson, courtesy of Vaunda Micheaux Nelson, p. 32. Sign backgrounds: © Lou Oates/Dreamstime.com, © iStockphoto.com/enviromantic, © iStockphoto.com/LordRunar, © iStockphoto.com/ShaunWilkinson.

THE HOUSE OF **COMMON SENSE** AND THE HOME OF **PROPER PROPAGANDA.**

THIS HOUSE IS PACKED WITH ALL THE FACTS ABOUT ALL THE BLACKS ALL OVER THE WORLD.

BOOKS WILL HELP HIM CLEAR THE WEEDS AND PLANT THE SEEDS SO HE'LL SUCCEED.

DON'T GET TOOK! READ A BOOK!

NOBODY CAN GIVE YOU FREEDOM. NOBODY CAN GIVE YOU EQUALITY OR JUSTICE OR ANYTHING.... YOU TAKE IT.

If you don't know and you ain't got no dough, then you can't go, and that's for sho.